Paulding

A Broadside for the Times

Paulding

A Broadside for the Times

ISBN/EAN: 9783744732116

Printed in Europe, USA, Canada, Australia, Japan

Cover: Foto ©Andreas Hilbeck / pixelio.de

More available books at **www.hansebooks.com**

A

BROADSIDE FOR THE TIMES;

BY

E PLURIBUS UNUM.

———⸰✦⸰———

New York:

JAMES O. NOYES, PUBLISHER,

No. 25 Howard Street.

1861.

A BROADSIDE FOR THE TIMES.

SHOTS.

SECESSION.

What is there in the name of STATE,
  The name of STATE, my friends,
So potent, so divinely great,
  That there begins, and ends,
      Authority?

What is SECESSION? 'Tis a claim
Of power in one only name:
Nation is nothing—country less—
Those letters five the all express:

    What is there in the name of STATE,
      The name of STATE, my friends,
    So potent, so divinely great,
      That there begins, and ends,
          Authority?

Whence comes this doctrine ?   Where its root,
That buds and blows, and bears such fruit ?
Its seed is in the plotter's brain,
And there for aye should it remain :

> What is there in the name of STATE,
> The name of STATE, my friends,
> So potent, so divinely great,
> That there begins, and ends,
> Authority ?

Why not a county ?—looking down,
Why not a precinct, parish, town ?
Why can't we all secede at will ?
Why not each individual ?

> What is there in the name of STATE,
> The name of STATE, my friends,
> So potent, so divinely great,
> That there begins, and ends,
> Authority ?

SHARE AND SHARE.

——

"Come, let's divide ! Come, let's divide !"
In haughty tone the Southron cried :
    " We'll take the niggers, we'll take the niggers,
        And leave the worn-out rag ;
    We'll pull no triggers, we'll pull no triggers,
        For Liberty, the hag !"

" And is it so ?   And is it so ?"
Replied the Northron in a glow :
    " Take you your niggers, take you your niggers,
        And of your bargain brag ;
    Leave us poor beggars, leave us poor beggars,
        Content with the dear old flag."

" See the Palmetto broad displayed ;
The nations nestling in its shade :
        Take you the buried memories
            That we will now forget,
        That lived on lands, and lakes, and seas,
            And 'round your banner met."

"See that, our banner, blooming fair,
Whose glories ye no more can share :

We'll take the ancient memories
　　We never can forget ;
Free hearts are fixed in love of these—
　　They are not buried yet."

———•••———

THE CRISIS.

THOUGH trade be dull, and credit low,
Though stocks and bonds do fall,
　　　　Pooh, pooh ! 'tis nothing—no—
　　　　Nothing at all, at all.

Though women's hearts beat thick and slow,
Though tears, from bearded men, appal,
　　　　Pooh, pooh ! 'tis nothing—no—
　　　　Nothing at all, at all.

Though Empires totter to and fro,
Though Peoples on their Maker call,
　　　　Pooh, pooh ! 'tis nothing—no—
　　　　Nothing at all, at all.

Though threatened with a blood-red woe,
Though horror front us like a wall,
　　　　Pooh, pooh ! 'tis nothing—no—
　　　　Nothing at all, at all.

BLOOD AND THUNDER.

——

I HAIL from the North, and I hail from the South,
    I hail from everywhere ;
I am to be known by the froth of my mouth,
    My wild and angry stare.

        I never can breathe but in a cloud
          Of pleasant smoke of powder—
        Complain that the cannon roareth loud !
          I wish it roared much louder !

I've kindred and kith, I have a good many,
    And if we have no brains,
We shouldn't be blamed, for we never had any,
    And naught from naught remains.

        I never can breathe but in a cloud
          Of pleasant smoke of powder—
        Complain that the cannon roareth loud !
          I wish it roared much louder !

Ye talk but of compromise, talk but of time—
    (Why waste so much of it ?)
Ye prate of opening civil war, as crime ;
    I want a touch of it :
      1*

I never can breathe but in a cloud
  Of pleasant smoke of powder—
Complain that the cannon roareth loud !
  I wish it roared much louder !

––––––––•◆•––––––––

A VIRGINIA ABSTRACTION.

WHEN your own State secedes,
  Or may secede ere long,
It curious questions breeds,
  Of moral right or wrong :

    Fill, fill your pockets, boys—
      Iago knew the world :
    Who cares for scruples !—toys
      We have behind us hurled.

When brooks are muddy, fish ;
  The trout can then be caught :
In troubled times, why, pish !
  These trifles go for naught :

Fill, fill your pockets, boys—
Iago knew the world :
Who cares for scruples !—toys
We have behind us hurled.

What men would honor call
In view of common life,
Is honor not at all
In view of coming strife :

Fill, fill your pockets, boys—
Iago knew the world:
Who cares for scruples !—toys
We have behind us hurled.

Sometimes the bottom's up,
Sometimes the wrong is right ;
Then heap with gold the cup,
And heap it with your might :

Fill, fill your pockets, boys—
Iago knew the world :
Who cares for scruples !—toys
We have behind us hurled.

THE POOR WHITE FOLKS.

———

THREE poor white folks sat on a stump ;
　Each whittled a chip of pine ;
Each chewed upon a pitchy lump—
　And on it he did dine.
The future gave fancy a plentiful scope,
And thus number one uttered every man's hope
　"Tom shall be governor, of course,
　　And Josey sit as judge ;
　And I'll command a troop of horse,
　　Or not a step I'll budge."

　　　　CHORUS—Rankitanki, Rankitanki,
　　　　　　Rank-tank-tank !

In sorry plight the poor folks sat ;
　Each one his hunger nursed ;
And as he thought of feeding fat,
　Each not a little cursed :
But still the bright future gave plentiful scope,
And thus number one uttered every man's hope
　"Soon darkies shall be cheap as dirt,
　　As dirt be darkies cheap,

And I go for't, and I go for't,
And I will buy a heap."

CHORUS—Rankitanki, Rankitanki,
Rank-tank-tank !

Somehow the present suited not
Each gaunt and ragged fellow ;
There was no bacon in the pot,
And every face was yellow :
But still the bright future gave plentiful scope,
And thus number one uttered every man's hope :
" Damn applejack—damn dirty work !
Old Bourbon is the stuff !
Our slaves shall dig, we'll live like Turk,
And fight, for fun, enough.

CHORUS—Rankitanki, Rankitanki,
Rank-tank-tank !

Lo ! by the stump there stood a shape,
And sadly eyed the three,
And they looked at the form, agape,
As gravely answered he ;

For now the dark future gave plentiful scope,
For him to disparage each poor fellow's hope :
    "You'll die, still drinking applejack—
      For you no darkies cheap—
    Judge, Captain, Governor, alack !
      You'll still your stations keep."

        Solo—Rankitanki, Rankitanki,
           Rank-tank-tank !

    The poor white folks to work now fell,
      But, to their great surprise,
    The tarred and feathered criminal
      Fast faded from their eyes ;
But still, as he faded, the future gave scope,
For him to disparage each poor fellow's hope :
    " Enough of fighting may be done,
      But you will play no pranks;
    As food for powder, all your fun
      To foot it in the ranks."

        Solo—Rankitanki, Rankitanki,
           Rank-tank-tank!

YE REMORSIFULL CONSPYRATORE.

———

" I FEAR that cleverer men than I—
(Poor men are always clever)—
That wanted place and wages high,
Have fixed my flint forever."

" If niggers fall and taxes rise,
    What will become of us ?
If corn is bought, and cotton lies,
The freight unpaid, and credit flies,
    'Twill finish some of us.
            I fear that cleverer men than I—
                (Poor men are always clever)—
            That wanted place and wages high,
                Have fixed my flint forever."

" They told me I was sore oppressed ;
    I didn't so clearly see it,
But thought I'd go it blind—the rest,
The wisest, bravest, poorest, best,
    By Heaven sworn—so be it.
            I fear that cleverer men than I—
                (Poor men are always clever)—
            That wanted place and wages high,
                Have fixed my flint forever."

" I had as much, in slaves and land,
    As one man could attend to :
I don't exactly understand,
Although the argument was grand,
    Why I the breeze should bend to.
        I fear that cleverer men than I—
           (Poor men are always clever)—
        That wanted place and wages high,
        Have fixed my flint forever."

"They told me that I soon would see
    My prospects insecure—
That my investments would not be
Worth half so much, ere long, to me—
    I find it so, for sure :
        I fear that cleverer men than I—
           (Poor men are always clever)—
        That wanted place and wages high,
        Have fixed my flint forever."

" Sometimes my thoughts are troubled—when
    I see the harm I've wrought :
I miss the former times—for then
I stood up, like a man, 'mongst men,
    And dared speak what I thought.

I fear that cleverer men than I—
(Poor men are always clever)—
That wanted place and wages high,
Have fixed my flint forever."

———◦◦———

EL EXTENSIONISTIBUSTERO.

—

WITH fifty thousand men in print,
With fifty thousand men,
We'll sweep o'er all the continent,
Nor be contented then.

Chu chu !
Chu chu !
Biz !
Fiz !
Whiz !

[*Excuse me, ladies and gentlemen, but a little steam* WILL *leak out.*]

What though we have but funds suspicious !
We've dreamed about an isle—
The wealthy CUBA—and Mauritius—
And all those islands so delicious—
And there we'll make a pile.

With fifty thousand men in print,
With fifty thousand men,
We'll sweep o'er all the continent,
Nor be contented then.

Chu chu !
Chu chu !
Biz !
Fiz !
Whiz !

What though our credit still declines
Into a deeper ditch !
There is a country that adjoins—
Silver and gold are there—the mines
Of MEXICO are rich.
With fifty thousand men in print,
With fifty thousand men,
We'll sweep o'er all the continent,
Nor be contented then.

Chu chu !
Chu chu !
Biz !
Fiz !
Whiz !

[*Excuse me, ladies and gentlemen, but a little steam* WILL *leak out.*

If then our conscience be not sore—
(Some think it is diseased)—
There's Walker's land, and several more
That lie along THE ISTHMUS shore,
    All ready to be squeezed.
      With fifty thousand men in print,
        With fifty thousand men,
      We'll sweep o'er all the continent,
        Nor be contented then.

            Chu chu ! Chu chu !
              Biz ! Fiz ! Whiz !

We'll take the leg of mutton next ;
    I'll pause for no details ;
We'll take it ALL, on some pretext,
From Panama, to where 'tis vexed
    By the Antarctic gales.
      With fifty thousand men in print,
        With fifty thousand men,
      We'll sweep o'er all the continent,
        Nor be contented then.

            Chu chu ! Chu chu !
              Biz ! Fiz ! Whiz !

se me, ladies and gentlemen, but a little steam WILL *leak out.*]

We'll plant the darky for a crop,
  Where'er the land agrees ;
Nor even after this will stop :
No, no : spin on, O humming top !
  We then will EUROPE seize.
    With fifty thousand men in print,
      With fifty thousand men,
    We'll sweep o'er all the continent,
      Nor be contented then.

        Chu chu ! Chu chu !
          Biz ! Fiz ! Whiz !

FOR THE UNION.

WHAT ! Halve each ancient monument
  Of fame in peace and war !
What ! Halve, (in common glory blent),
  The gleam of every star !
    I'm for Union, I'm for Union,
      And never, never I
    Will give up Union, give up Union,
      Till I die, till I die !

What ! Halve the cheer that UNION pealed,
  The war-cry of the free !
What ! Halve the flag of every field,
  That blazed in every sea !
    I'm for Union, I'm for Union,
      And never, never I
    Will give up Union, give up Union,
      Till I die, till I die !

What ! Halve the blood so freely shed
  O'er all the lands and waves !
What ! Halve the laurels of the dead,
  Uprooted from their graves !
    I'm for Union, I'm for Union,
      And never, never I
    Will give up Union, give up Union,
      Till I die, till I die !

What ! Halve the due respect that clung
  'Round every man, abroad !
What ! Halve the hope that ever sprung
  Where'er his shadow trod !
    I'm for Union, I'm for Union,
      And never, never I
    Will give up Union, give up Union,
      Till I die, till I die !

PROPHETIC!

I.

THE PEOPLE'S PRESIDENT.

In the first days of Union, those
That were in truth THE PEOPLE, chose
    For themselves a President :
Firm in the chair he took his seat,
And ruled the state with mind discreet,
    On justice aye intent ;
Began, and so continued once begun,
Laying the strong foundations, one by one,
    On which a nation's rights could stand ;
All faction's sting of faction's force bereft ;
And, when he left the seat, behind him left
    Increasing glory, and a *growing* land.

II.

THE POLITICIANS' PRESIDENT.

But years rolled on, and, day by day,
The people less bore real sway,
  Their faithless servants more ;
Till these, the while the masses toiled for gold—
(As the Imperial chair of Rome was sold)—
  The Presidency bargained for :
From bad to worse thus on it went,
  Until, by intrigue bare,
The POLITICIANS put *their* President
  Into the curule chair.
Straight he began, continued once begun,
Sapping the strong foundations, one by one,
  On which a noble fabric rose,
And made of all his powers misuse,
And played he fast, and played he loose,
  Now with his friends, and now with foes,
  But still relaxed his clasp
Of the great sceptre given him to hold,
Until at last that mighty sceptre rolled—
  Rolled from his nerveless grasp :
And so there passed from his disastrous hand
A waning glory, and a *lessening* land.

III.

MORAL.

[N.B.—*Not only of this Shot, but of the whole Broadside.*—E. P. U.

Sure as the stars shine in the skies,
Unless the honest PEOPLE rise,
   On reformation bent,
And, by their need, or by their choice,
Demand, gain, hold, and *use* a voice
   In their own government,
Ere many years have passed away,
When we have had our anarchy—
(And we shall have it)—a great cry,
   From inland vale and ocean shore,
Will go up to the Lord on high :
   " GIVE US AN EMPEROR !"